baby GIRAFFES

KATE RIGGS

CREATIVE EDUCATION • CREATIVE PAPERBACKS

ENTS

I Am a Calf 4

Dropped to Earth 6

Hairy Horns 8

I Am a Young Giraffe 10

Speak and Listen 12

Calf Words 14

Reading Corner 15

Index 16

I AM A CALF.

I am a baby giraffe.

I was six feet (1.8 m) tall at birth. I could stand, walk, and run within an hour.

ossicones

I have hairy "horns" on top of my head. These are called ossicones. My coat has spots.

My mother feeds me milk. Then I start eating plants.

I love acacia leaves! My neck is growing longer. At my first birthday, I will be 12 feet (3.7 m) tall.

I am a young giraffe!

UUUHNG!

Can you speak like a calf? Giraffes can hum, snort, hiss, and grunt.

Listen to these sounds:

https://www.youtube.com/watch?v=w618jriMW0M

Now it is your turn!

CALF WORDS

acacia: a tree or bush in Africa that has yellow or white flowers; giraffes eat its leaves and twigs

mane: the longer hair on a giraffe's neck

ossicones: hornlike parts on a giraffe's head that are covered with skin and fur

READING CORNER

Bell, Samantha S. *Meet a Baby Giraffe*.
Minneapolis: Lerner, 2016.

Kelley, K. C. *Baby Giraffes*.
North Mankato, Minn.: Amicus, 2018.

Schuetz, Kari. *Giraffes*.
Minneapolis: Bellwether Media, 2012.

INDEX

coats 8

eyelashes 5

family 7, 10

food 10, 11

manes 5

necks 11

ossicones 8

size 6, 11

sounds 13

spots 8, 9

PUBLISHED BY CREATIVE EDUCATION AND CREATIVE PAPERBACKS
P.O. Box 227, Mankato, Minnesota 56002
Creative Education and Creative Paperbacks are imprints of The Creative Company
www.thecreativecompany.us

LIBRARY OF CONGRESS CATALOGING-IN-PUBLICATION DATA
Names: Riggs, Kate, author.
Title: Baby giraffes / Kate Riggs.
Series: Starting out.
Summary: A baby giraffe narrates the story of its life, describing how physical features, diet, habitat, and familial relationships play a role in its growth and development.

Identifiers: ISBN 978-1-64026-247-8 (hardcover)
ISBN 978-1-62832-810-3 (pbk)
ISBN 978-1-64000-388-0 (eBook)
This title has been submitted for CIP processing under LCCN 2019938404.

CCSS: RI.K.1, 2, 3, 4, 5, 6, 7; RI.1.1, 2, 3, 4, 5, 6, 7; RF.K.1, 3; RF.1.1

COPYRIGHT © 2020 CREATIVE EDUCATION, CREATIVE PAPERBACKS
International copyright reserved in all countries. No part of this book may be reproduced in any form without written permission from the publisher.

DESIGN AND PRODUCTION
by Chelsey Luther and Joe Kahnke
Art direction by Rita Marshall
Printed in the United States of America

PHOTOGRAPHS by Alamy (Peter Mundy, Christian Musat, PA Images, JUAN CARLOS MUÑOZ ROBREDO, Lorraine Swanson), Getty Images (Sean Gallup/Getty Images News), iStockphoto (Musat), Shutterstock (Justin Black, Bohbeh, Hein Myers Photography, Eric Isselee, SasaStock)

FIRST EDITION HC 9 8 7 6 5 4 3 2 1
FIRST EDITION PBK 9 8 7 6 5 4 3 2 1